EARTH'S
NATURAL
BIOMES

GRASSLAND BIOMES

Louise and Richard Spilsbury

WAYLAND
www.waylandbooks.co.uk

First published in Great Britain in 2017 by Wayland

Copyright © Wayland, 2017

Editor: Hayley Fairhead
Design: Smart Design Studio
Map (page 9) by Stefan Chabluk

ISBN: 978 1 5263 0135 2
10 9 8 7 6 5 4 3 2 1

www.hachette.co.uk
www.hachettechildrens.co.uk

Printed and bound in China

All photographs except where mentioned supplied by
Nature Picture Library www.naturepl.com
p4, title page and back cover(r) Gerrit Vyn; p5 and imprint page(t) Denis-Huot; p6
Jeff Vanuga; p7 and imprint page(b) Denis-Huot, p8 and title page(l) De Cuveland
/ ARCO; p9 and back cover(l) Wild Wonder of Europe / Lesniewski; p10 (main) Neil
Lucas; p11 and p31(t) David Welling; p12 and title page(t) Paul Johnson; p13 Ben
Hall; p14 Pete Oxford; p15 Luiz Claudio Marigo; p16 Wim van den Heever; p17 Klein
& Hubert; p18 and p30 Ingo Arndt; p19 Rolf Nussbaumer; p20 and front cover(tl)
Kim Taylor; p21 Denis-Huot; p22 Laurent Geslin; p23 and front cover (tr) Anup Shah;
p24 and front cover(br) Jamie Robertson; p25 Constantinos Petrinos; p26, contents
page(t) and cover main Anup Shah; p27 Denis-Huot; p28 Shattil & Rozinski; p29,
contents page(b) and p31(bl) Kristel Richard.

Photographs supplied by Shutterstock: p10 (inset) Chase Clausen;
p12 (inset) HGalina.

CONTENTS

WHAT ARE GRASSLANDS?

Grasslands are wide, open areas of land that are mainly covered in grasses. As the wind blows through them, some grasslands look like giant seas of grass.

Seas of grass

Grasslands are found in places where there is just enough rain for grasses to grow, but too little rain for many trees to survive. As well as grasses, grasslands are also home to flowering plants, such as clovers and sunflowers, and shrubs, such as yuccas.

Grasses all have thread-like roots and long, thin leaves, but there are many different kinds of grasses in grasslands. For example, big bluestem grass can grow to three metres tall. It has blue-green stems with purple or green seed heads on top. Ryegrass is a short, tufted green grass and wild oats are medium-height grasses with dull brown stems and seed heads.

This is a grassland in Kansas, USA, with the spiky leaves and tall stems of a yucca shrub in the foreground.

Amazing Adaptation

Adaptations are special features or body parts that living things develop over time to help them survive in a biome. Grass plants have roots that spread deep and wide below the surface to collect enough water to survive dry spells.

Buzzing with life

Grasslands may look like huge, dull fields of grass, but they are buzzing with life. Millions of worms, ants, beetles and other animals live among the grass roots underground. Insects eat grasses and seeds above ground. Birds eat seeds and make nests from dry grass. Birds, reptiles and other animals eat plants, insects and each other.

Greedy grazers

The vast areas of grass also provide food for large animals, like zebras. Grazing animals like these spend up to 18 hours a day eating to get enough nutrients from grass. They are often seen together in large herds or groups. While some animals in the herd are feeding, others can keep a lookout for predators, like lions.

Lions may sneak up on a herd slowly before starting a chase across this grassland in Kenya.

Fact Focus: Biome or Habitat?

Biomes are regions of the world that have a similar climate, plants and animals, such as deserts, forests, rivers, oceans, tundra and grassland. A habitat is the specific place in a biome where a plant or animal lives.

DIFFERENT GRASSLANDS

There are many different grasslands around the world, but they can be split into two main kinds: temperate and tropical.

Temperate grasslands

Temperate grasslands are found in places that have warm summers, cold winters and very little rain all year round. These biomes may have scattered trees, but there are not enough to slow down or block the wind, so they can get very blustery.

Grasses stop growing to survive the cold winters in temperate grasslands. They store water and food in their roots and save energy until the warm, damp spring comes. In spring and summer, they grow new stems, leaves and flowers and the sound of swishing grasses fills the air.

This temperate grassland in Wyoming, USA, gets covered in snow in winter. Bison can clear away snow with their massive heads to find grass to eat underneath.

Fact File: Hortobágy National Park

Location: Puszta, Hungary
Size: 820 square kilometres
Overview: The largest temperate grassland in Europe, home to butterflies, hamsters, polecats and saker falcons.

Tropical grasslands

Tropical grasslands are found in parts of the world that have two seasons: rainy and dry. Very heavy rains fall in the rainy season, which is why tropical grasslands tend to have longer grasses and scattered bushes and trees. Rains form watering holes that animals can drink from. During dry seasons there is little or no rain. Most plants turn brown and stop growing. They rest until the rainy season arrives. Then the plants and flowers grow rapidly again.

Tropical grassland trees have defences to stop animals eating them. Acacia trees have big, sharp thorns. But a giraffe can squeeze its extra-long tongue between the thorns and curl it around leaves to pluck them off.

Amazing Adaptation

Grasses keep on growing even after being nibbled down by hungry animals. This is because they grow from their base, near to the ground, rather than from their tips as trees do.

The giraffe's long legs and neck help it to reach tasty leaves at the top of tropical grassland trees.

WHERE ARE THEY?

There are either temperate or tropical grasslands on every continent of the world, except Antarctica. In fact, about one quarter of the Earth's land is covered with grasslands.

Tall, fluffy pampas grasses give their name to pampas grassland.

Temperate grasslands around the world

Temperate grasslands have different names in different places. The wide, flat grasslands of North America are known as prairies. Prairies have taller grasses in wetter areas and shorter plants in drier parts. Steppe grasslands are the biggest in the world. They stretch from eastern Europe to central Asia. It is colder and drier than the prairies, so other plants are scarcer here. Pampas is very flat grassland between the Atlantic Ocean and the Andes Mountains in South America.

Fire!

One feature that is common to grasslands all over the world is fire. In hot summers and dry seasons, wildfires spread quickly in old, dead grasses that are very dry and catch alight easily. Fires actually help grasslands because grasses grow back soon after a fire, as long as their underground roots survive, but most trees and other plants are killed. This is another reason there are so few trees in grasslands.

This falcon is hunting animals running from the flames as a grassland fire burns.

Amazing Adaptation

In Australia the woody seed cases of some banksia trees only open in a fire. The seeds have lots of space to grow after a fire and ash from the fire acts like a fertiliser.

Arctic Ocean

North America

Europe

Asia

Atlantic Ocean

Africa

Pacific Ocean

Pacific Ocean

South America

Indian Ocean

Australia

Temperate grasslands
Tropical grasslands

Antarctica

This map shows where the temperate and tropical grasslands of the world are. Grasslands are often found between areas of desert and forest.

9

PRAIRIE LIFE

Prairie plants and animals have different strategies for surviving the challenges of fierce wind, heat, and lack of water in the prairie grassland.

Prairie wildflowers provide nectar and seeds for insects, birds and butterflies, like this Monarch butterfly.

Prairie plants

Some plants, such as ironweed, have short, tough stems to help them cope with strong winds. Many grass stems are thin and can bend in the wind, springing back up after it has passed. Indian grass and other plants grow roots up to 4.5 metres deep to get enough water.

Amazing Adaptation

Prairie rattlesnakes are coloured green and brown for camouflage, so they can sneak up on unsuspecting prey on the grassland.

Prairie animals

Crickets, wild turkeys, wolves and many other animals live on the prairie. Prairie dogs are small, chubby animals that live in large groups. They work together to dig out huge burrows using sharp claws. They escape predators and harsh weather by hiding in tunnels underground.

Prairie dogs bite off tall plants above their burrows so they can spot predators sneaking up on them. If one prairie dog spots danger, it cries out and the others race underground to take cover.

The heaps of mud left by the prairie dogs' digging make useful lookout posts. Prairie dogs are so called because their warning cry sounds like a bark, but they are really a kind of squirrel.

A deadly bite

Prairie dogs can dive underground to escape eagles and wolves, but long, thin prairie rattlesnakes can slither after them into their hidey-holes. The rattlesnake has two long, hollow teeth called fangs. These deadly weapons can inject venom into prey to kill it. Prairie rattlesnakes often live in prairie dog burrows in winter when it gets very cold. If this happens, prairie dogs have to dig new burrows!

STEPPE LIFE

It's dry in the steppe grasslands and although warm in the daytime and in summer, it gets very cold at night and in winter. The saiga antelope and the fierce steppe eagle are both perfectly adapted to life in this dry, chilly biome.

The saiga's eyes are at the end of bony knobs on either side of its head. They help it spot wolves and other predators coming from the side as well as from behind.

Nosing about

The saiga's nose is so long that it hangs down over its mouth. This special snout has bones, hairs and mucus inside that help to filter out dust in the dry summers. It also warms up the cold air a saiga breathes in during snowy winters to stop the animal getting too cold.

Like many other grassland grazers, saigas have long legs and hard hooves on their feet. Hooves help grazing animals run fast on hard ground to escape danger. Saigas can run up to 130 kilometres an hour — that's faster than a car on the motorway!

Fact Focus: Steppe Plants

Most grasses in the steppe grow less than 50 centimetres tall. The tough, thorny brambles and other shrubs living here are also short, to keep out of the path of icy winds.

Eagle-eyed predator

The steppe eagle, like many grassland birds around the world, mainly hunts from the sky. It soars over open land, watching for prey, before diving down at speeds of up to 300 km an hour. It grabs and kills small animals, such as wild hamsters, in its powerful talons. Then it rips its prey apart with its strong hooked beak, or swallows them whole if they are small enough.

Steppe eagles can be lazy too! They sometimes wait by burrow entrances to catch animals when they come out.

The steppe eagle has excellent eyesight. Its eyes are so big that they take up most of the space in its skull.

Fact File: The Kazakh Steppe

Location: It covers about 60 per cent of the country of Kazakhstan.
Size: 804,500 km²
Overview: One of the largest steppe regions, home to saiga antelopes and wild horses.

PAMPAS LIFE

It's warm and windy in the pampas grasslands, with dry summers. There are few trees, but some areas of pampas are moister than many grasslands so they have very tall grasses. The flat lands of the pampas are also home to some unique animals.

A sticky situation

Termites are ant-like insects that use chewed-up mud and saliva to build huge mounds. These mounds set hard like rock when they dry. The giant anteater uses its strong front legs and claws to break holes in these termite homes. Then it pokes its long, narrow snout into the holes.

Inside its long snout, the anteater has a tongue that is 50 cm long. It is also very sticky! The anteater shoots its tongue in and out very quickly, catching termites before they can get away and gobbling them up.

Giant anteaters can eat up to 30 000 ants and termites every day. Their long hair protects them from angry termite bites.

Fact Focus: Pampas Plants

Pampas grass (see page 8) grows in large, thick clumps. This shades the ground around the grasses and stops other plants growing close to them that would steal their water.

Expert hunter

The maned wolf hunts for small animals at night or in the dim light at dusk and dawn. Its long, thin legs help it to see over the tall pampas grasses and its huge ears help it to hear small sounds. It can twist and turn its ears to work out exactly where an animal, like a rabbit or guinea pig, is hiding underground.

When a maned wolf hears prey in a burrow, it taps the ground with one of its front paws. This scares the animal so it runs out and then the waiting maned wolf pounces!

The maned wolf gets its name from the thick, dark mane of hair on the back of its neck that stands up when it senses danger.

Amazing Adaptation

Many pampas animals burrow into the ground to escape the heat and predators like the maned wolf. One owl (see page 28) even builds its nest in underground burrows.

SAVANNAH LIFE

The savannah grassland has scattered trees and a variety of grasses, from the deep-rooted Bermuda grass to elephant grass, which can grow to three metres tall. Many large animals live and feed on savannah plants, including the elephant, the largest land animal in the world, and the ostrich, the biggest bird on Earth.

Trunk tricks

An elephant spends about 16 hours a day eating grass, leaves, twigs and bark. Its long, flexible trunk can wrap around a branch and snap it off or even push over a tree. The trunk also has two pointed parts at the end that work like fingers. They can grasp and remove a single leaf and pop it into the elephant's hungry mouth.

Elephants also use their trunks to suck up dust from grassland soils and spray it over themselves. This helps to prevent sunburn and blocks heat from the Sun.

A layer of dust reduces the number of insect bites and stings an elephant receives in the savannah.

Big bird

Ostriches walk slowly around the grassland eating grasses and other plants and sometimes insects too. Ostriches peck up and swallow sand and small stones. These help to grind up the plant foods in their stomach. They lift up their long neck to hold their head high to look out for predators. Their heads may be small but their eyes are as big as cricket balls, so they can see to the front and sides.

The ostrich has wings but it cannot fly. Instead it has very long legs that it uses to run quickly away from danger. Ostriches can run twice as fast as humans!

Ostriches use their strong, long legs to run from lions, wild dogs and hyenas or to kick them away.

Fact File: Serengeti

Location: Tanzania and Kenya
Size: 14,763 km²
Overview: Animals that live here include lions, hyenas, cheetahs, giraffes, rhinos, zebras and warthogs as well as many birds, insects and reptiles.

BORN SURVIVORS

Grassland animals have some amazing ways to make sure their young stay safe and survive in the biome.

Safety first

After a baby kangaroo (a joey) is born, it's only about the size of a peanut. It crawls into its mother's comfy pouch, where it drinks milk and grows quickly. The joey stays in the pouch for at least four months. It's safe from predators in the Australian grasslands as its mother can hop quickly away from danger. Even after the joey leaves the pouch, it still dives back in for safety or when it is tired until it's about a year old.

Amazing Adaptation

A kangaroo mother has muscles in her pouch, so she can make it go floppy to tip the joey out! She can tighten the pouch to hold on to the joey when in danger.

If a kangaroo senses danger, she can hop away at up to 48 km per hour with her baby safely tucked inside her pouch.

A smelly start

Dung beetles are found in grasslands all over the world. The babies are called larvae and they have a very unusual and slightly smelly start to life! Dung beetle parents collect dung and roll it into balls that can be as big as an apple. They then work hard to push the dung balls into an underground burrow. The female lays an egg inside each dung ball. The larvae that hatch out of the eggs have an instant meal because they eat their way out of the dung balls. The adult beetles also feed on dung.

Dung beetles have spikes on their legs to grip the dung balls and roll them along.

Fact Focus: Waste Disposal Experts

Dung beetles help grasslands. Burying balls of dung helps to recycle nutrients back into the soil and stops grasslands from being covered in dung left by many grazing animals.

EAT OR BE EATEN

The lives of all grassland plants and animals are linked together in different food chains. Food chains tell the story of who eats who in a grassland biome.

The first link in the chain

Grasses are the first link in the food chain because they make their own food. They trap the Sun's energy in their leaves and use it to combine water with carbon dioxide, a gas in the air. This makes food in the form of sugars. The process is called photosynthesis. Plants store some food in their bodies to use later and use the rest to grow.

Every link in a food chain relies on each other. Grass needs sunlight to grow. Rabbits need grass to survive. If there are lots of rabbits, foxes have plenty to eat.

Fact Focus: Food Webs

Several food chains together form food webs. For example, on a prairie a mouse eats grasses and grasshoppers and is eaten by coyotes, owls and snakes.

Hungry predators

Other grassland animals feed on the plant-eating animals to get the energy they need to survive. Lizards and snakes eat insects and rodents. Cheetahs catch gazelles, and lions and hyenas work in teams to bring down large grazers, such as zebra. Eagles and other birds of prey swoop from the sky to snatch small grazers while they are eating.

Amazing Adaptation

The cheetah's long legs help it run fast and its long tail helps it steer and change direction, to help it catch fast-moving prey in the grassland!

In one food chain, a gazelle eats grass and a cheetah eats the gazelle.

Full circle

After an animal dies, worms and tiny bacteria in the soil help to break down dead animal bodies and waste. When these living things digest and break down animal bodies they return nutrients to the soil. These nutrients help plants to grow and new food chains to form.

ANIMALS ON THE MOVE

Many grassland animals migrate long distances to find food. Saiga antelope travel 1,000 km north to wetter parts of the steppe for summer and return south in autumn. The sight of two million wildebeest, gazelle and zebra migrating across the Serengeti is one of nature's greatest wonders.

Lines of migrating wildebeest can be 40 km long.

A dangerous journey

Rain falls at different times of the year in various parts of the Serengeti savannah. So, herds of grazing animals migrate up to 3,000 km to follow the rains and find enough grass to survive. It is a dangerous journey. Lions chase the herds and at river crossings there is the risk of crocodile attacks. Zebras and wildebeest often travel and feed near each other for safety. Zebras have good eyesight and wildebeest have great hearing.

Born to run

Many wildebeest and zebras have their young while travelling on migration routes. During the rainy season there is more grass for the young animals to eat. Wildebeest calves can stand and run within minutes of being born.

Zebra foals are born feet first. Their legs are almost as long as an adult zebra's and they can walk and even run within an hour. The young animals need to be able to keep up with the herd or they could end up as a hungry predator's lunch.

Each zebra has a unique set of stripes and a zebra foal learns to recognise its mother's stripe pattern so it can easily follow her in the migrating herd.

Amazing Adaptation

Some scientists think that the stripes of all the zebras in a herd blend together to confuse lions so that they have trouble picking out one zebra to chase and attack.

GRASSLAND PEOPLE

More people live on grasslands than on any other biome in the world. Grasslands also feed more people than any other biome.

Fields of grass

Grassland soils are ideal for growing crops or raising livestock. Instead of wild grasses, many areas of grassland have been replanted by people with other grass-like plants that they and their animals can eat, such as corn, wheat, rice and other grains. There are also vast areas of grassland where farmers and ranchers raise huge herds of farm animals, such as sheep and cattle.

Amazing Adaptation

Grasslands have healthy soils because when their many underground roots die, bacteria and other decomposers release nutrients from them. This helps other plants to grow.

Ranchers round up huge herds of their cattle that roam across enormous areas of land in the grasslands of Queensland, Australia.

Home on the biome

As the world's population increases, people are spreading further and further into grasslands. Grasslands are often on flat areas of land that are easier to build on; grasses are easier to remove than thick forests, and many of these biomes also have a climate people can live in. By building their houses, offices, factories or even parks and golf courses on grasslands, they destroy grassland habitats.

On safari

People also enjoy visiting grassland biomes, such as the savannah, to see the wildlife. This gives tourists a better understanding of grasslands and their animals and makes it more likely that they will help to protect them. The money tourists pay can help people protect areas of savannah. But tourist jeeps can damage grasslands and crowds of people can disturb animals and stop them feeding or breeding.

Safari vehicles crowd into an area near the Mara River so tourists can see wildebeest and zebra during the Serengeti migration season.

Fact Focus: Disappearing Prairies

Only about one per cent of the North American wild prairie grasslands still exist. Most have been taken over by people for farms or towns.

GRASSLAND THREATS

Grassland biomes look like tough, wild places but in fact they are fragile because water is so scarce. When grasslands are in danger, the wildlife in them is too.

Drying up

Cities and farms use large amounts of water. Farmers may also use strong chemicals to kill weeds that kill wild plants. Their huge numbers of goats and cows eat the grasses and pull them up by their roots. Without water and without plants to hold the soil together, the nutrient-rich topsoil dries up and blows away, and the land becomes dusty and bare.

Another problem is that global warming is making temperatures around the world increase. As parts of the world get hotter, the amount of rain that falls and when it falls also changes. Grasslands are already short of water so this increases the risk that grasslands will dry up completely.

If watering holes dry up, grassland animals like these thirsty lions may not be able to get enough water to survive.

Animals under threat

When grasslands lose their plant life, or people take over grasslands for farms or towns, animals have nothing to eat and nowhere to live. Animal food chains get broken. If there is not enough grass to support large numbers of grazing animals like zebras, there will not be enough food for animals, such as lions, that eat the grazers.

Animals face other dangers, too. Some are treated as pests to stop them from eating crops. Farmers have killed about 98 per cent of all prairie dogs to stop horses and cows being hurt by falling into prairie dog holes. In the savannah, people catch and kill animals, such as cheetahs and rhinos, for their fur or horns.

People kill rhinos for their horns, which are then crushed and used to make traditional medicines.

Fact Focus: Endangered Animals

Human actions in grasslands have left many animals in danger of becoming extinct, or dying out forever. Endangered grassland animals include cheetahs, African wild dogs, and black rhinos and many more.

GRASSLAND FUTURES

Grasslands are very special biomes that are home to some of the world's most amazing animals, so people are working hard to protect them for the future.

Scientists gently attach bands to burrowing owls to track their movement through the grassland.

Expert advice

Scientists study grasslands and their wildlife to understand what they need to survive and how to help them. For example, grasslands need some fires to stop too many trees growing, so scientists advise people who manage grasslands to allow controlled fires to burn rather than putting them out.

Caring for the land

People are also learning how to care for the soil and grasses. They protect and restore areas of water, which grasslands need to survive. They plant trees around the edges of grasslands to act as windbreaks to stop the topsoil blowing away. Farmers help by allowing an area of land to recover before letting livestock graze it again.

National parks

Governments turn some areas of grassland into national parks. This protects them by law. People can visit to enjoy the wildlife and scenery, but they cannot disturb or harm the animals or their habitat. No hunting is allowed and there is a limit on the number of roads that can be built or the amount of water people can use.

Taking action

You can help to protect grasslands too. You could adopt an endangered grassland animal. The money you pay helps people to protect those animals. Or, you could write to governments to ask what they are doing to help to protect the world's grasslands or the grasslands in your country. You could learn more about grasslands and their wildlife and tell other people about how important these biomes are.

Wild Przewalski's horses were bred in zoos and then released back into their natural habitat to avoid extinction.

Fact Focus: The Last Wild Horses

Przewalski's horses are the last of the world's truly wild horses. They were in danger of becoming extinct, until they were brought back to Hustai National Park in Mongolia.

GLOSSARY

adaptation special feature or way of behaving that helps a living thing survive in its habitat.

bacteria tiny living things that can cause diseases or decompose waste.

biome large region of Earth with living things adapted to the typical climate, soils and other features. Tundra, grasslands and deserts are types of biome.

breeding having young.

camouflage colour, pattern or shape that makes it hard to identify an object against the background it is in.

climate typical weather pattern through the year in an area.

continent one of the seven large masses of land on the planet: Asia, Africa, North America, South America, Europe, Australasia and Antarctica.

crop plant grown for food.

decomposer living things, such as bacteria and fungi, that break down bits of dead plants and animals and waste into nutrients plants can use to grow.

digest break down food into nutrients, usually inside the stomach and intestines.

Equator imaginary line around the centre of the Earth

extinct when every individual plant or animal of a particular kind has died out.

filter pass something through a device with tiny holes to remove unwanted material.

food chain way of showing animals that eat each other as links in a chain, from plants that make food through to living things that turn waste into nutrients for plants to grow.

food web feeding relationships between living things, usually in a particular habitat or biome.

global warming rise in average temperature of Earth caused by human use of machines and electricity, which is altering weather patterns worldwide.

grazing feeding on grass.

habitat place where an animal or plant typically lives.

hooves hard covering over animal toes

larvae stage in development that some animals go through before becoming adults.

livestock farm animals

migrate move from one place to another, normally in search of something.

mucus slimy substance sometimes called snot.

national park an area in nature where the wildlife is protected by law.

nutrient substances living things need to live and grow.

photosynthesis process by which green plants make sugary food using the energy in sunlight.

predator animal that catches and eats other animals.

prey animal eaten by another animal.

recycle to make something new from something used before.

reptile a snake, lizard or other animal that has cold blood, lays eggs, and has a body covered with scales or hard parts.

rodent animal with large front teeth for gnawing, such as a mouse or a rat.

roots underground parts of a plant that take in water and nutrients from the soil.

talons bird claws

topsoil top layer of soil that contains the nutrients plants need to grow.

venom poison some animals can make in their bodies and use for defence or to kill prey.

watering hole pool of water from which animals regularly drink.

FIND OUT MORE

Books
Grasslands (Amazing Habitats)
Leon Gray
Franklin Watts, 2016

Grassland Ecosystems (Ecosystems of the World)
Pam Watts & Melissa Higgins
Core Books, 2016

Grassland Food Webs in Action
(Searchlight Books: What Is a Food Web?)
Paul Fleisher
Lerner Classroom, 2015

Grassland Animals (Animals in Their Habitats)
Sian Smith
Raintree, 2014

WEBSITES AND WEBCAMS

You can see videos, facts and images about grasslands at:

www.bbc.co.uk/nature/habitats/temperate_grasslands,_savannas,_and_shrublands

Watch the animals that visit a watering hole in grasslands at:

explore.org/live-cams/player/african-watering-hole-animal-camera

Find out more about threats grasslands face and what is being done to protect them at:

www.worldwildlife.org/habitats/grasslands

INDEX